Up Went the Goat

Written by
Barbara Gregorich

Illustrated by
Robert Masheris

Up went the goat.

5

The goat saw a coat.

The coat was too big
for the goat.

The goat saw a boat.

The goat was too big
for the boat.

Down went the boat.

Down went the goat.

Good night, goat.